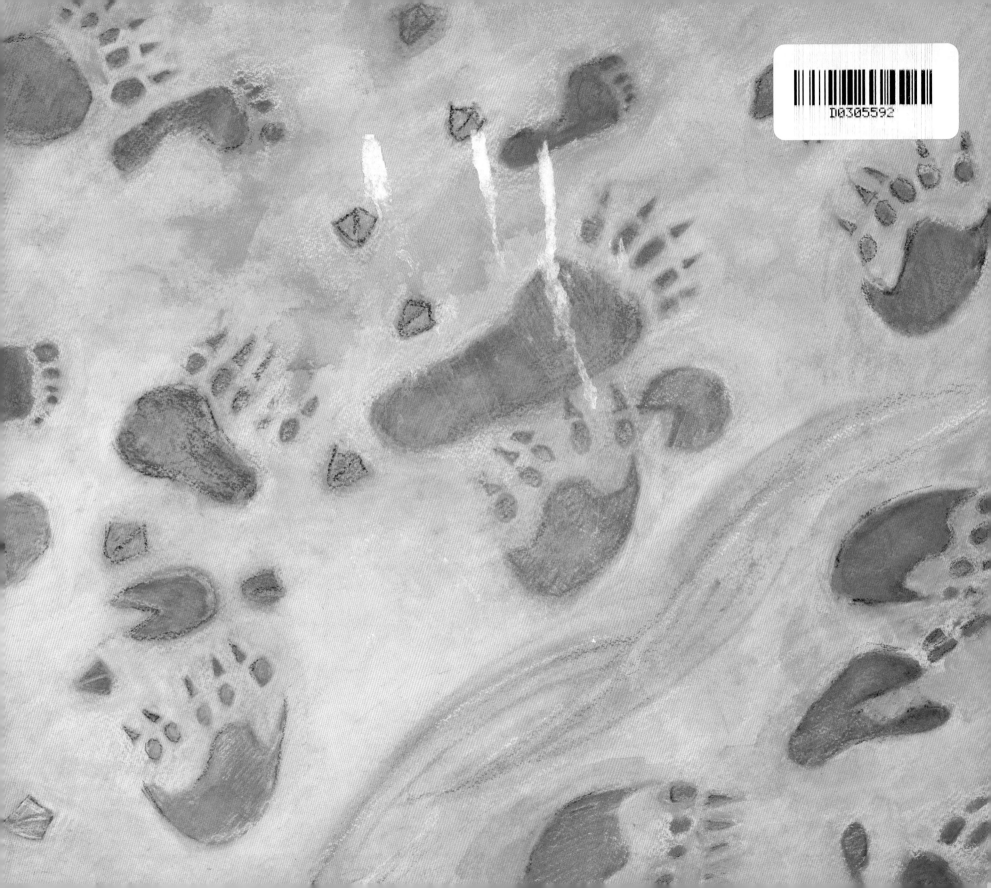

First published in Great Britain in 2000 by
Frances Lincoln Limited, 4 Torriano Mews,
Torriano Avenue, London NW5 2RZ

British Library Cataloguing in Publication Data
available on request

ISBN 0-7112-1504-9

Printed in Hong Kong

1 3 5 7 9 8 6 4 2

Ellie's growl

Karen Popham

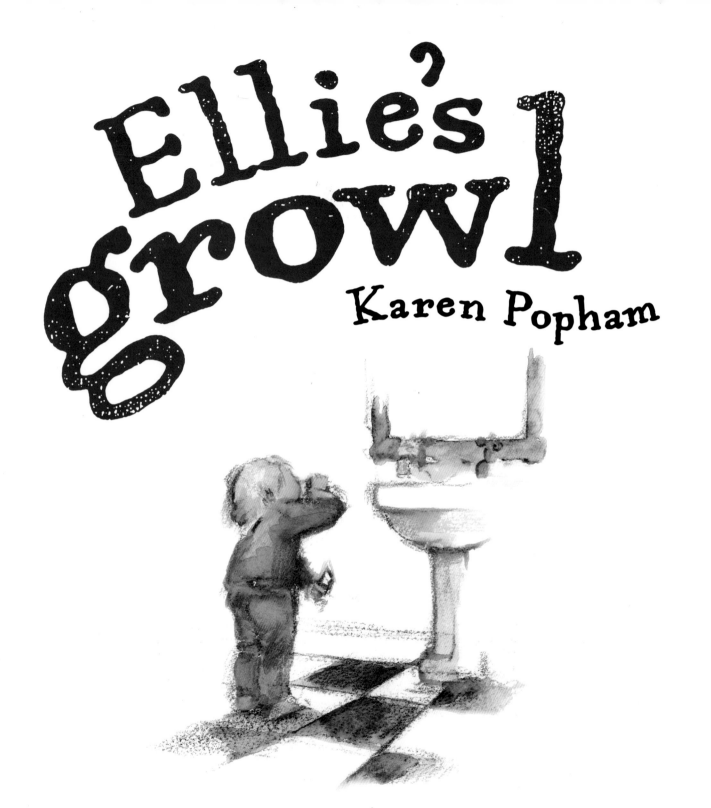

FRANCES LINCOLN

For Christopher – K.P.

Ellie likes her bedtime books, especially stories about animals. She likes it best of all when her big brother William reads them to her, because he makes wonderful animal noises.

William can make the sound sea lions make
when they **challenge** each other.

He can **flap** and **spit** like an angry swan,

whinny like zebras jumping,

and
croak
like courting toads.

William **blusters** like polar bears swimming,

he can **SSSS** like a snake when it's slithering,

and **beat** his chest like a baboon does...

...when it's in the mood.

He can even **sing** like the great blue whale.

One evening William reads
Ellie a jungle story.
And when the tiger prowls...

...William **growlS!**

Next morning, while she is cleaning her teeth,

Ellie **growlS!**

Ellie likes growling.

After breakfast she **growls** at the dog.

The dog hides.

After lunch she **growls**

at a little boy.

The boy howls.

After tea she **growls** at a cow.
The cow walks away.

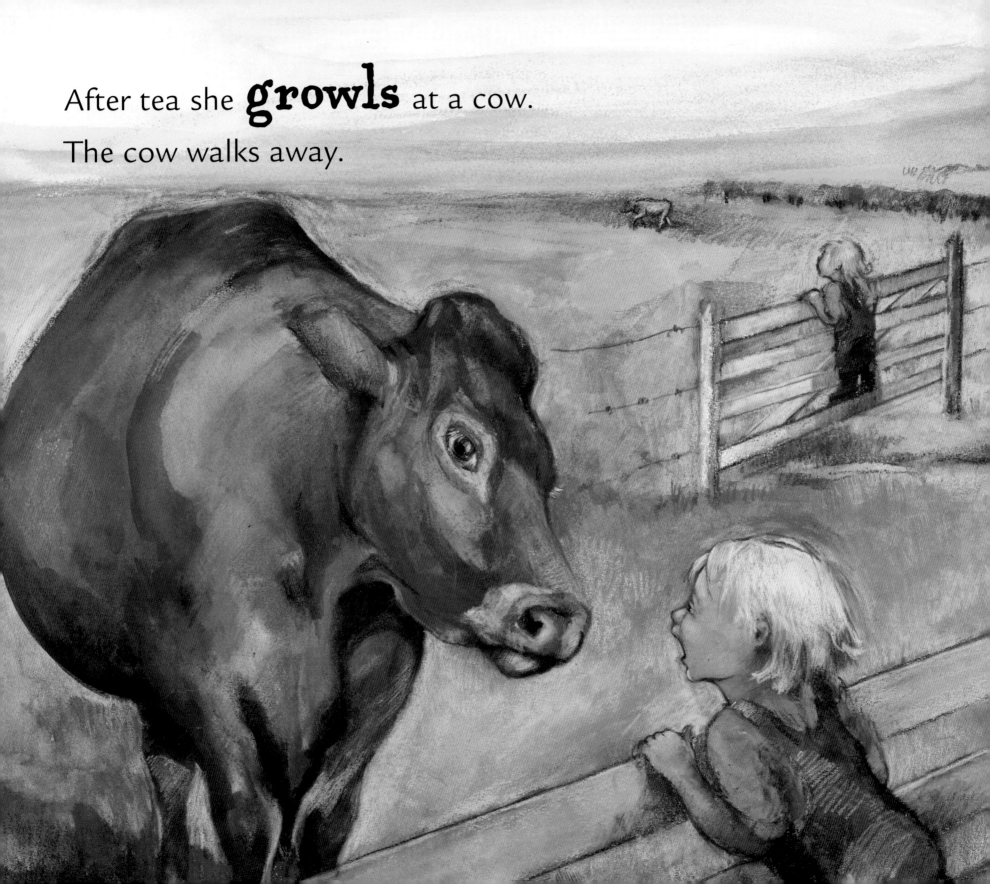

At bath-time Ellie **growls** at William.

William gets cross.

At bedtime
she **growls**
at the kitten.
But the kitten...

...**growlS** back!

Ellie cries.

The kitten comes and nuzzles her and begins to purr. Ellie listens carefully, then she tries to purr too,

and William comes in...

...to read them both a story.